A RUDE STORY

RICHARD B.C.

Copyright © 2024 RICHARD B.C.

All rights reserved.

ISBN:9798339859277

DEDICATION

To Lydia.
Be all you can be.

ACKNOWLEDGMENTS

I have to thank the Universe for aligning the stars in a manner that would allow me such a great support system. When it was dark your lights illuminated my path. Kayla, you are appreciated. Jake, you are my first positive role model. Mahogoney, couldn't have written this without the laptop you gifted me. Mom, Dad, Paul and Ebony, family is life.

PROLOGUE

    The Wild Wild West was a different time inning of itself. It is primarily known for being a time of lawlessness but it is most renowned for the infamous outlaws that helped earn its moniker. Outlaws like Billy The Kid, Jessie James, Doc Holiday, and Wyatt Earp are well known outlaws that are written about often but that isn't who this story is about. Racism and slavery was a big part of the early colonization of America so a lot of colored people were not given credit for their contributions to the country. That includes the negative aspects as well.
    There were black outlaws. We live in a different time so you may have begun to hear about the black outlaws that walked back then. It's beginning to become more talked about but the historians are leaving out the most infamous of them all. This story is about the most feared outlaw to ever walk the Wild Wild West. He was so feared that people have tried to erase his name from the history books all together. They almost succeeded but traces of him are still there. His legend has only survived due to many generations of consistency when it comes to oral traditions.
    This story is about the Buffalo Soldier himself. His name was Rude Boy Dread. He is widely remembered for the thirteen long dreadlocks atop his head. Rude Boy Dread was most known as being the leader of a gang of outlaws called The Rude Boys. He was notorious for challenging other outlaws and proving his superiority as a top bad man. It is even believed that outlaws like Billy The Kid purposely avoided crossing paths with him. That story is for another time. This is an origin story and it is about the birth of the infamous outlaw Rude Boy Dread.

CHAPTER 1

    Within Houston, Texas there is a small town known as Blackwood. The small town isn't much, like most other towns in the west during this time. The state is in its early stages of being settled. Lawlessness and criminal activity is common in these parts becoming the chief reason the area has become known as the wild wild west. At that time Blackwood only consisted of a bar, a sheriffs office, a bank and the homes of its founders. Most of its establishments were not even two decades old yet. The small town had virtually just been born.

    The small town was void of all movement except for a tall fair skinned man with short scraggly black hair atop his head. He was wearing long faded blue jeans and a dirty white collared shirt. His face was worn with age and his eyes looked weary. His slow gait was methodical. He swiftly moved along the dusty dirt road. He moved with purpose as he made his way towards the bank which lies at the heart of the little town. He walked through the wooden swing doors entering the bank. He took a quick scan of the small building as he stood in its entrance. The bank was empty save for the bank teller behind the counter, a wannabe guard, and a young black boy that was busy sweeping at nothing.

    The man stomped his heels against the floor knocking most of the dirt from his boots. The young black boy rushed over to sweep up the dirt as the man made his way to the bank teller. The guard silently nodded at the man. Blackwood was so small that everyone knew everyone. Hearing the man's footsteps as he approached, the teller looked up from under the spectacles he wore. A smile spread across his face as he set down the feather he had been writing with. He placed it back into the container of ink beside him.

    "Blackwood. What do I owe the surprise?" The bank teller greeted the town's founder.

    "Just doing my rounds and please call me Winston. Look George, I'm tired of telling you the same thing everyday." Blackwood replied.

    "You tire yourself. I don't plan to change anytime soon. I call you by your surname sir. That's all. It's a sign of respect."

A RUDE STORY

Blackwood exhaled deeply and tilted his head towards the ceiling in surrender. The release of air sounded like the hiss of a rattlesnake. He chuckled heartily at the bank teller's comment.

"Sure keeps this place clean." Blackwood commented as he glanced around again, changing the subject. He visited the bank often and he couldn't remember a time when the bank wasnt clean. It was all just small talk. "I was unsure when your mother first came to me asking to let you run the place once it was finished being built , but now I see my daughter-in-law is a fine judge of character."

The bank teller beamed with pride.

"Place is clean, isn't it?" He smiled. "As long as Brown keeps sweeping like he's supposed to, the place stays clean like I like it to. Brown! Come here boy!" He yelled suddenly to the young black boy who had been sweeping. Brown responded immediately. The young black boy had a caramel skin complexion. He had a small afro of dark black hair on his head. He was wearing ripped blue jeans and a burgundy collared shirt that was one size too big for him. Brown kept his eyes to the floor as he stood before Blackwood and the bank teller.

"He's trained well and he's doing a good job with the place. You know it's hard to find good help these days. He wasn't here yesterday." Blackwood stated as he observed him.

"Just got him from the Dumont Plantation. Only cost me fifteen cents and I got that on credit at that. I only put a penny down."

Blackwood nodded in agreement with him. It was a good deal. He would have plenty of time to make the money to pay for the slave.

"Get back to work boy!" The teller suddenly yelled at Brown. He startled him so good that he tripped on nothing as he headed back to where he had been earlier before Blackwood had walked into the bank. "Who told you to stop sweeping? I don't want to see a speck of dust in this place. You make me look bad and I'm gonna make you look bad. You know what I'm saying? I ain't gonna tell you again."

Brown frantically began sweeping as if to let him know he was doing just as he had been told. The teller chuckled then he leaned towards Blackwood and whispered so only his ears could hear as if he had something top secret to say.

"Can't let that boy get too comfortable or he'll get lazy so I keep him on his toes. Keeps the place up to par." George boasted.

"I see you're still writing." Blackwood said changing the subject yet again as he indicated the ink and feather that was alongside the piece of parchment that the tellers elbow rested on.

"Oh this? Just a little poetry. You know me and my poetry." The teller said as he began to fiddle with the edges of the parchment. "I'am no Christoper Colombus but I am talented nonetheless if I do say so myself. Care to hear some?"

Blackwood attempted to tell him no but the young blonde haired man had already begun to read to him. Blackwood looked annoyed as he read his poetry but he stood there and endured. No one in the small bank noticed the small group of men walk in. Blackwood and the teller were preoccupied with the teller's poetry. Although Blackwood was annoyed, he still was listening. He had nothing else to do anyhow and he had to admit that it was actually good.

The guard was lost in his thoughts. He was thinking to himself about the fun he would have when he got home to his wife. They had only just recently married and he was already having visions of a future where they had eight beautiful children. They had one in the oven now and seven more to go. He was anticipating the procreation process. Brown was still sweeping as if his life depended upon it.

Three black men all with long dreadlocks sauntered in through the entrance of the bank cooly. They moved with an air of confidence about themselves. They were clearly organized. The largest and darkest skinned of the trio stopped in the entrance blocking it off. He stood at six feet and easily weighed two hundred and seventy-five pounds. Stopping at his shoulders his dreadlocks were the shortest out of the trio. He turned his back to the inside of the bank and crossed his arms above his chest as he began to watch the streets outside. He lightly brushed his jacket to the side so he could let his hand rest on the pistol at his waist.

"Mon knows the drill. Give me the money and nobody gotta get hurt." The heavily accented voice came from the tallest of the trio. The tall, slim, brown skin complexioned man stood at six foot seven. His long dreadlocks were tied behind him in ponytail fashion. They stopped about midway down his back. He had a potato sack in his right hand and he was brandishing a revolver in his left hand as he moved. He pointed it at Blackwood and told him not to make any funny moves as he climbed onto the counter. Blackwood looked utterly surprised that a stranger was in his bank let alone a black man. The fact that they were being robbed shocked him too. Maybe more than the sight of a black outlaw, the likes of which he had never seen before.

The teller took one look at the pistol in the outlaws hand. Reality didn't register for him immediately. The tall man shoved the potato sack into his hands and told him to fill it through gritted teeth. He

A RUDE STORY

considered refusing for only a brief moment. The tall man kept his pistol trained on him the entire time and he pulled the hammer back on the revolver as if he had read his mind. That got his undivided attention. He immediately began to do as he was told, filling the potato sack with the little money that the small bank had. It wasn't worth losing his life over. He had never fired one before plus the other two men were armed as well. One glance provides him with that information. He loaded the potato sack slowly as if waiting for something or someone to save the day. The tall man immediately tells him to speed up and he does just that.

The guard has his sights on the tall man as he robs the teller. His hand is slowly dropping to the pistol at his hip

"Don't try it."

The calm commanding voice freezes the guard in his tracks. It came from behind him. He cursed himself for not being more aware of his surroundings. The tall man had been the first disruption he noticed. Instead of inspecting the rest of the bank he had gone into tunnel vision and the tall man had been the only thing he saw. He hoped if he saved the day that the sheriff would have no choice but to make him a deputy which was what he really wanted. He wasn't even really a guard. He had purchased his own pistol and was volunteering his services in the bank to show that he could be of use.

The sheriff had denied his attempt to become a deputy calling him incompetent because he had accidentally discharged his pistol out of nervousness into the floor of the sheriff's office during his interview. He had been so excited that he was about to get the position. He still couldn't recall what had caused his firearm to go off. He wondered what type of name the sheriff's imagination would use to bash him when he heard about what was taking place.

The guard looked towards the direction the voice had come from. He saw a man with a brown skinned complexion. He stood at 5'11 feet and had an athletic build. A navy blue colored paisley handkerchief was tied around his neck. His black beard was long and filtered with gray hairs that hinted at wisdom, considering how young the man looked to be. A quick glance around the room allowed the guard to realize that there were three robbers in the room. All of the men had dreadlocks but this one had the longest hair of them all. His hair stopped just below his waist. He had never seen hair like theirs before but that wasn't what he was looking at. The man's right hand was hovering calmly just inches above the pistol in the holster at his waist.

"Reach and you a dead mon. Ya hear? Me don't tell wunna twice." The man taunted him. The guard noted that the men spoke with a strange accent that he couldn't place his finger on. Although it had a British ring to it, he could tell it was some form of slang that almost made him not understand what was being said. Body language was universal though so he knew that his life was being threatened by the man's stance and the look in his eyes.

The guard may not have been the sharpest knife in the cutlery but he knew it wouldn't be wise to make any moves. He was clearly outnumbered. Three guns to one. He didn't like those odds. Plus the look in the black man's eyes in front of him told him he wasn't playing. They say the eyes are the window to the soul and one look was all he needed. This was a man who had taken souls before and would again if he felt it was necessary. He was skilled in the use of pistols unlike the guard who was a novice. He had experience shooting and prided himself on his aim but he had never shot another human before. He had definitely never been in a shootout and he wasn't trying to see if he could survive one. Going out in a blaze of gunfire wasn't an option either. It wasn't like he would get to enjoy the fame in the afterlife. He only wished to make sure he made it home to his wife who he had been daydreaming about before they entered the building. He lifted both his hands in surrender and watched the man with the blue handkerchief that was obviously the gang leader.

The man smiled and it wasn't a sinister smile. It was very charismatic in fact. The smile stretched from one ear to the other at the sight of his surrender. He began to slowly and calmly saunter over to him. He walked with an air of confidence that could easily be mistaken for arrogance which wasn't the case. The man was actually very meek and humble. Those that knew him would say they had never seen him angry before. He was always composed and in control. His voice had a sort of melody to it that almost made you think he was singing.

"Smart. You are a smart one." He told him as he stopped in front of him. He lightly slapped him on the cheek. " I don't care what they say about wunna."

The guard appreciated the compliment but didn't understand the last part. Was this outlaw aware of him and his misfortunes? Had he heard the bad talk about him that was circulating through the small town of Blackwood or was he just reading him like an open book. He couldn't help his face from frowning as the gang leader relieved him of his firearm. He took it from him and placed it into his waistband at his back.

"You don't need this." He told him. "You are a smart mon. Why make me dead you about the money? Wunna never get the chance to spend the money. Me spend the money." The man punctuated his last sentence with his billion dollar smile. Then he glanced to a corner of the room where slight movement had caught his eye. He saw the young light skin complexioned boy crouching down in the fertile position. His hands were still tightly wrapped around the broom. It looked as if the boy was cowering in fear. His head was tucked in between his knees. Something about the little black boy drew him near.

"Hey little fella." The gang leader called to him as he slowly approached him. Brown peeked up at him. "What do you do here around all these pale skins?"

Brown saw the gun at the man's hip and tucked his head back between his knees.

"It is rude not to look a mon in the eyes as he speaks to wunna. Ya hear?"

Brown slowly lifted his head until he was looking into the gang leader's eyes. He didn't know what to expect. He had never seen any black men like this before. They had hair like he had never seen before and they had just done what he had never seen black people do before. They had defied the white man. Not just that, they had made the white man submit to their wishes. The only times he had ever seen blacks defy white people had ended badly for the blacks.

Something about these blacks were different though. These were men of power. They had to be very bad men to put fear into the whites. If this man wanted him to look into his eyes then it was very clear to him that he ought not to defy them. It wouldn't be wise to ignore the commands of such a powerful man. He tried not to seem afraid as he created eye contact with the man. He tilted his chin up.

"Rude boy." The gang leader observed as he spotted defiance in the little boy's demeanor. He leaned back and got a better look at the young black boy. He felt as if he could see a hint of aggression that had been buried in the boy's subconscious. To the average eye it wasn't nothing but not to him. He was much accustomed to violence and he knew what he saw. The boy had potential in him.

"Oh!" He exclaimed, getting the attention of everyone in the building. They all looked at him. "Slim! Look at the lickle rude boy." He tilted his head in the direction of the young black boy in indication that it was him who he was talking about. Slim, the tallest and skinniest of the gang was the one collecting the money from the teller. He glanced at the young black boy with the broom. The onceover he gave him was full of judgment. He rolled his eyes before bringing his attention back to the teller who was almost done filling the potato sack.

"Him not a rude boy. The boy broke I tell you. Look at him again." Slim told him.

Brown didn't know what Slim meant by calling him broke but he had a feeling it wasn't a good thing to be. He felt it had something to do with his status as a house slave. He dropped his head again when the gang leader looked back at him.

"Look at me, my youth." He told Brown. He waited until he was looking into his eyes again before he continued to speak. "Who treats you better? The pale skins or your own people?"

The question stumped Brown. He was unable to answer. It wasn't that the question was a difficult one that stumped him because it was simple. The blacks treated him better and they showed him a love that he had never been able to experience from the whites save for the little boy named Johnny who had taught him to read. Even their friendship had been in secret. He felt that there was more in the question the black man had asked him. Plus he didn't even stick around waiting for an answer as if the question had been rhetorical. He wondered what the true purpose of the question had been. He almost asked what the point of the question had been, but Slim's announcement cut him off before he got a word out.

"I have the money! Let's get out of here." Slim yelled. He was already jumping down from atop the counter to leave. He was moving towards the exit with the potato sack over his shoulder like he was Saint Nick. The biggest man was the first to exit the building and the gang leader was the last to leave the bank. He paused in the entrance and straightened the handkerchief around his neck and winked at the guard before leaving.

Brown Didn't know what to think. He didn't know if what he had just seen had really happened or not until the guard cursed aloud. He had never seen men of color who possessed as much power as those men had. He was still trying to make sense of the question. He couldn't help wondering if the man had been offering him some sort of asylum. Who would treat him better, he had asked. The answer was simple but he knew there was more to it. Yes, the three men were strangers but he couldn't help thinking the gang of blacks would treat him better. He couldn't even imagine the quality of life they were experiencing.

"Brown!" The bank teller yelled, getting his attention. He had been completely consumed by his thoughts. "What do you think you're doing boy?"

It was only then that he realized he had been heading to the exit. It was as if his legs had a mind of their own. He knew he was likely to never again see black men like he was seeing. He didn't want to be telling stories about how he had seen them later. He preferred to act upon his sights. He knew if he didn't it would be something he regretted for the rest of his life. He glanced back and saw the bank teller's face twisted in an angry sneer. It only motivated him to move his feet faster. He dropped the broom and ran for the exit as fast as he could.

   He didn't even know what he was really doing. He was acting upon impulse. He knew he had to do something although he didn't know what that something was. He ran so fast that he wasn't paying attention as he bumped into the gang leader as he exited the bank. The man was solid so he wasn't affected by the collision in the same manner that Brown had been. He was nearly knocked from his feet. He shook his head to remove the stars from his vision.

   The man turned to face him. Brown looked into the man's dark brown eyes expectantly. He just had to go with them. He would much rather leave with the black outlaws who were strangers to him, rather than staying amongst the white people who were his oppressors. Even though he lived better than the average slave, he was still a slave.

   "Rude boy." The man called him as he smiled at the boy's actions. "You like to come with The Dreads?" He asked him already knowing what his answer would be. Brown nodded his assent quickly.

   "No way!" Slim yelled as he mounted his brown mare. "The boy broke. He will only slow us down. The life we live is too much for him to handle. It will be like bringing a fish to live upon the land. Leave him."

   Brown shot Slim a look of defiance but inside he was afraid. He was afraid of what might happen to him now if they didn't take him with them. He hadn't thought about it when he had made his move because he knew he hadn't had time to think. Opportunities like these were once in a lifetime and he knew he had to take the risk. The risk was definitely great. He would surely be punished severely for his attempt to leave even if he had only made it to the outside of the bank. He had seen runaway slaves tortured once they were caught. He had even seen one tortured to death before. He visibly winced at the thought which didn't go unnoticed by the gang leader.

   "The boy has shown heart. He comes to us against the pale skin's wishes. That action alone shows me where his heart is at. It is with the people where it belongs. He may not know what the life we live is about but he obviously is willing to learn so i think he deserves the chance to do so. Puma has spoken." The gang leader stated. "Plus we can't leave the youngblood now. Imagine what the pale skin's will do to him now that he has revealed his hand."

Now it was Slims turn to visibly wince. He glanced over at the big man with them. The largest man of the gang continued to sit upon his large black stallion in silence. He solemnly nodded his agreement to Pumas statement. His face was filled with compassion for the boy's situation. Slim finally exhaled a breath of air as he conceded. He didn't like the idea of bringing Brown along but he didn't protest anymore either. He watched as Puma climbed onto his white and black spotted stallion, then he outstretched his hand to Brown who didn't hesitate. He pulled him onto the horse so that he was sitting behind him and then they all rode off out of town. Brown didn't look back, not once.

CHAPTER 2

    Rude Boy was sore in the bottom from attempting to keep his balance as he rode the horse behind Puma. He clinged onto him as if he was holding on for dear life. He had never ridden before today, let alone even seen blacks that rode horseback before the gang. They were truly a sight for sore eyes. One may even call them a black man's dream, and that's only if a black man had enough imagination to think men of their caliber into existence. He had heard stories of free blacks but he had never in his wildest dreams conceived men like these, who commanded the power and respect as they did. It was all very new to him. The gang seemed to be riding off into nowhere. His inner compass was going haywire. He had no idea where he was at or where they were going but he assumed it was all a part of the new life he was pursuing.
    No more of life in the town of Blackwood. Living in Blackwood was better than living on the plantation he had been born on but something told him that the life he would live amongst Puma and his gang of outlaws would greatly outshine any possibilities at either of the places he knew. He appreciated the change of scenery. He took in all the sights around him like a sponge. From the bright orange-red sun in the sky to the different shrubs and cactuses. What would look like nothing for miles to others, looked like a beautiful painting of art to him. He was grateful to be free. He had always dreamed of being free since he could remember but now he was and it hasn't come about the way he thought it would have.
    Suddenly the gang halted and they all began to dismount their horses. Rude Boy was left holding onto the horse as if he could fall at a moment's notice. Slim watched him as he shook his head. "Yeah the horse loves you too but it's a male horse if you didn't know. I think you're starting to make him feel awkward hugging him the way you are." He laughed at his own joke.
    It quickly became apparent to him that no one was going to help him down. No one was even looking his way. They had all begun small tasks. Even Slim. He fought his way down by sliding from the back of the horse. Inch by inch. He earned a small chuckle from

A RUDE STORY

Slim just as his feet touched the ground. His face was up against the horses behind as he clung to it and Slim found the sight just humorous. He laughed even harder when Rude Boy let go and pushed away from the horse.

Puma, the gang leader, had one foot propped up on a small boulder. It was then that he realized that there were several small boulders setup in a circle that numbered the number of people in the gang before he had shown up. In the center of the circle was a much smaller circle of rocks that he easily recognized as having earlier been used for a fire. He had not known why they had suddenly stopped at first but now he knew why. This was the gang's camp. The largest man of the group had sat down on one of the boulders and was gazing up into the sky. The sun would be setting anytime now. Slim was done clowning him and now he was playing a small harmonica he had produced from his pocket.

"Blue. Go collect some fresh firewood and get a fire started before the sun goes down. These sand gnats are nasty especially during sundown but they don't like the smoke." Puma instructed the largest man in the gang whose name was clearly Blue before turning to Slim. "I'm going to take care of some business and I'll take Rude Boy with me."

"I'll go catch dinner." Slim told him as if he was beating him to the punch. "I don't need my horse while I'm hunting so you can let Rude Boy ride it. Your probably going to have to teach him how though. Be gentle with my mare." He smiled before jogging off. Rude Boy didn't know why it felt so good to hear Slim refer to him as Rude Boy but it did. Maybe it was because Slim had originally been against him tagging along with them. It wasn't the name itself. It was more about the character associated with it. The name had a sense of respect over it that he had never sensed around his birth name. Its use made him feel at home as if he wasn't amongst strangers that he had only just met not more than twenty-four hours ago.

"Come on now brethren." Puma told them as he easily jumped up onto his horse. He watched Rude Boy patiently as he got up onto Slim's horse with no assistance. The horse moved back and forth anxiously as he struggled to get atop it. It took him a few tries but he eventually was able to do so. It actually seemed easier to him getting onto the horse versus when he had got off. Puma didn't scoff or ridicule the process one time. He simply waited expectantly until the task was completed. Rude Boy exhaled a breath of exhaustion as he leaned against the neck of the horse to get rest.

"Follow me." Puma told him before taking off suddenly. Rude Boy didn't even know how to tell the horse to move but it was clear that his teacher would be trial and error. He told the horse to go but it ignored him up until the point where he became frustrated to the point that he kicked the horse. The action caused the horse to jolt into a sprint that nearly knocked him from his seat on its rear. He luckily was able to get a grasp on the mane of the horse before falling. The horse ran so swiftly that he was forced to cling to it with all his might. He clung to the horse's neck desperately.

   Before he knew it, the horse had halted. It was only copying the horse it had been running alongside that also carried Puma. Rude Boy's arms were sore from the exertion he used to stay atop the horse. He was happy to finally reach their destination. He saw that they had arrived at a plantation that looks vaguely familiar to him. There was no way it could be the same one. He mentally denied the possibility that this could be a place he had been to before. They had traveled far. Maybe his mind was playing tricks on him. He was thirsty and hungry, he concluded.

   His thoughts were interrupted when a short, stubby white man suddenly came into his view. He appeared seemingly from out of nowhere. He had been leaning against one of the fence posts that marked the outer rim of the plantation. Spitting a glob of chewing tobacco from his mouth, he walked towards them as they approached. Rude Boy correctly assumed that the man had been waiting for them.

   "Howdy." The white man greeted the leader of the outlaw gang. His greeting was warm and friendly. It also came with a smile which perturbed Rude Boy because of the fact that Puma was an outlaw. Maybe the man didn't know that he was but there definitely was a feeling of familiarity in the greeting. He couldn't understand what they would have in common or why they would be dealing with eachother but he was sure that he would find out soon if he just payed attention.

   "Respect." Puma replied.

   The white man glanced at Rude Boy but after that he paid him no further attention. "You got the money?" He asked him.

   "You have the bacco?"

   "Let me see the money."

   "Me don't come here to play games with you mon. Show me the bacco." He demanded. He spoke with a no nonsense tone. The white man clearly took notice too because he didn't push the issue again. He turned his head to where another white man was approaching. This man was on horseback. "Here it comes now." He stated.

The second white man was wearing a black cowboy hat and unlike the first, a pistol was in his belt. His horse was coming toward them at a complete run. It kicked up a large cloud of dust as he brought it to a sudden stop. He spit on the ground in front of Pumas horse in a disrespectful manner. Rude Boy noticed the whip in the belt on the opposite side of the white man. He instantly recognized the man. It was Timmy. He was the Dumont Plantations nastiest overseer. He knew this because he had been born at this very plantation. He had suspected that this was the same plantation when he had first arrived but now he had the proof he was looking for.

Fear gripped Rude Boy. The feeling was so powerful that he had the urge to make his horse run as far as he could from there. He didn't know where he would go but he wanted to be anywhere but there at that moment. The only thing that kept him from doing just that, was the look on Puma's face just before he was going to take off. His visage resembled that of a lion. He looked fierce and without fear. He was cool, calm and collected and his aura of confidence began to rub off on him.

Memories of Timmy began to flood his mind as he laid his eyes upon him once again. He had witnessed him publicly punish the slaves at Dumont plantation on numerous occasions. His hands began to tremble unconsciously as he held onto his mare. He attempted to move behind Puma and his horse instinctively as his confidence slowly began to disappear just from being in front of a man he only knew for violence and hatred. Timmy's history of violence was only reinforced by the sneer on his face as he glanced at Puma. He meant to mug Rude Boy too but he wasn't able to get a good look at him because he was positioned behind the gang leader. There was something strange about the young black boy who seemed to be intentionally trying to avoid his eyes.

"Who's the little nigger boy in the back? What's he up to? Seems guilty of something if you ask me." Timmy said as he craned his neck as he tried to look around Puma to get a better look at Rude Boy. There was something oddly familiar about him. The first white man shrugged his shoulders as if he didnt care which was true. He could care less who the young black boy was. He was just trying to get the money and go. It was already as good as spent in his mind. He already knew what he was going to get with it. He had even written a list that showed what all he wanted. He was eager to start spending. Puma made his horse move so that its body would completely obscure his vision of Rude Boy. He wasn't blind to the man's attitude and the way he had disrespectfully spit in front of his horse. He was doing his best to overlook his actions so he could get what he came for but he wasn't going to let him dictate the meeting. He didn't come to kill anyone but he would do just that if this man's energy continued to rub him the wrong way.

"Don't fret about my Rude Boy. You want the money. Or no?" He threw the bag of gold coins onto the ground just in front of the two white men. The first white man quickly snatched up the bag and opened it to take a look at its contents. Timmy moved closer to him so he could get a look into the bag as well. They were both in awe over the amount of gold coins in the bag. They loved the way they shined in the moon's light.

"Sweet mother of sally, Timmy. We have hit the jackpot!"

"Let me see that." Timmy demanded as he snatched the bag from the other white man greedily.

"Give me the bacco." Puma commanded him sternly.

Timmy's face went from a smile to a sneer again. It was obvious he didn't like doing business with a black man. He believed that the entirety of the black race was inferior to the white race. He didn't care if the man was free or not. None of that mattered to him. Nothing could put a black man on equal standings with a white man in his opinion. He fumbled through his pocket before tossing a bag to the white man with him. He didn't want to even acknowledge what the black man said. He wasn't conversing with any blacks unless he told them that they had permission to speak, so he ignored him and let his friend hand over the small bag.

"It's all there." The first white man told him as he handed the bag to Puma.

"Better be or you will be seeing me again." Puma stated matter of factly. His threat caused Timmy's head to snap up at him and his anger flared. His pearly white face turned red in color. He was completely shocked at the audacity of the black man that he didn't even have a response. He wasn't used to hearing a black man speak like this one. He watched as the man with the strange hair turned and told the young black boy with whom he called Rude Boy to follow him. He wanted to say something but it had all happened so fast and they were already leaving at a full sprint horseback. He scowled at their backs as they rode off. Timmy watched the young boy who Puma had called Rude Boy glance back at him one last time giving him a clear enough look at his face for the first time.

"I knew it. That was Brown. That boy aint no free nigger." Timmy cried in exclamation.

"What are you crying about now Timmy? We got more money here then we ever had before in our life but you just got to find something to complain about. Cheer up. Look in that bag again. We are rich."

"Crying? That nigger just threatened us to our faces and you didnt say squat. Boy throws a couple gold coins around in your face and you act like it didn't even happen. What type of white man are you? You are a disgrace to the white race if you ask me."

This got his attention and even riled him up a bit. "Fuck that nigger." He replied impulsively as he shrugged his shoulders. "We rich. That stupid nigger just gave us more gold than the tobacco was worth. I'm talking ten times over easy. We won. Can't you see that?"

"How that nigger come across all that gold anyways? I've never seen that much gold in my life. It's all fishy if you ask me and I don't like the smell."

"Robbing banks." The first man stated as if it was a simple fact.

"Robbing banks? That's a crime. That would make him a god damn outlaw. I know you isnt trying to say we just did business with some sort of nigger outlaw?"

"That's exactly what I'm telling you."

"Why didn't you say something? Im thinking this was some sort of free nigger or something. We could have taken the money and turned him in to hang. I'm sure there's got to be a bounty on him if he is a real outlaw. That is a double win if you ask me."

"First of all, I tried to tell you but you didn't want to hear anything about him when I told you I was striking a deal with a black. Said you didnt want to hear another word about no nigger if i recall. Second of all, that nigger is a bad son of a bitch. Run with some gang called The Dreads. All of them are wanted outlaws and he is supposed to be the leader. That would make him the baddest of them all. They are wanted for everything from robbery to a multiple range of murders. I figured it's not worth running the risk of trying to kill them. It's not like ive ever killed anything more than a rattlesnake. Frankly, I'm trying to stay alive and enjoy all this gold. Maybe you need to take another look." He opened the potato sack for him to look into but Timmy shooed it away.

"No nigger ever killed me before. Just aint gone happen, I reckon. Are you one hundred percent sure these boys are outlaws?" Timmy asked him as his finger caressed the trigger of his pistol absently.

"Cocky son of a bitch told me so himself. Even gave me this when I met him." He reached into one of his pockets and retrieved a piece of paper from his pocket and then he handed it to him. Timmy unfolded the paper and sure enough it was a wanted poster that depicted three black men with dreadlocks. It referred to them as

'The Dreads' and the bounty said they were all wanted dead or alive. He recognized the man standing in the center of the trio. It was clearly the black man who had just stood before him. He balled the poster up in his hands before dropping it onto the ground and stomping it with his foot.

"Im going to get those niggers." Timmy vowed. He spoke more to himself just above a whisper. "Murder,Robbery and theft. Somebody has to stop them savages. They can't be allowed to run wild. If it has to be me who puts a stop to it then that's just what it is."

"Theft? That wanted poster don't say nothing bout no theft."

"They stole that nigger boy Brown. Boy used to be on my plantation. I'm in charge of the slaves on the whole plantation. It's like they stole the boy from me and I can't have that. They are going to pay and we are going to get paid at the same time. We can get our 'bacco back and the bounty. You think we are rich now. We are going to be the richest white boys in the whole of Texas. I'm talking about generational wealth here."

"I'm down." He agreed, letting greed rule his judgment. "So what do we do now?"

"Listen closely…" Timmy began.

CHAPTER 3

After about an hour and a half of traveling they came to an open plain. At the center of the plain was a multitude of teppe's. The teppe's were basically makeshift huts. Large branches tied together held up the leaves, grass and dried mud that made up the roofs. Smoke could be seen rising from the center of the camp. Rude Boy saw a number of light skin complexioned people moving throughout the camp. Indians. He had overheard the whites talking about them before. They claimed that the Indians were mindless killing savages who they often warred with. He wondered why they had come here now. The Indians were wearing clothes that were created from cured animal skins. The cured animal skins only covered their sexual organs. The rest of their bodies were exposed and they didn't wear shoes either. A party of the Indians was coming out to meet them as they approached.

The Indian chief was the only one of them that was riding horseback. His long black hair was braided and he had a feather behind his right ear and a crown made of feathers on his head. He wore necklaces that were heavily ornamented with animal teeth, shells and copper. He was surrounded by Indians that were the exact ideal image of what he might think warriors would look like. They had tribal ink on their bodies and faces. They all wielded sharp spears and a few of them leveled their spears in their direction before the chief said something in their native tongue that made them all visibly relax. Some of the Indians had bow and arrow as well.

"Friends, the Buffalo Soldiers are." The Indian chief said as he jumped off of his horse.

"Brethren. Thank you for welcoming us with open arms." Puma replied as the two leaders greeted each other with a firm hug.

"We have just returned from a hunt. My boy was successful at making his first kill. Look at what he has caught." The chief indicated a young boy behind him who moved to the front of their group. He was dragging along a boar that looked as if it weighed more than him. Its long tusks were deadly sharp. He struggled to pull it behind him but he didn't ask for help either. He had a big smile on his face that clearly spoke of the fact that he was proud of his kill. "Look at the size of the beast. He is only nine winters and already he shows the strength and courage of the blood that runs in his veins. He is a natural. He brings honor to his ancestors.

"What brings you to our humble place of life?" The chief asked him.

"I have tobacco I wish to trade with you."

"Tobacco? We could always use some more of it. What do you wish for?"

"Ganja."

"Gatunlati?" The chief said using the name they used for marijuana.

"Yes."

"Ok I see. The fragrance is quite sweet. I can understand your request. We've used it in our ceremonies for generations and we will continue for generations to come."

"Here." Puma said as he handed the chief the bag of tobacco. The chief took the bag before passing it to another Indian who tucked it away. Then he motioned to another Indian who came forward and handed Puma a bag. He brought his nose to the bag and deeply inhaled. The strong smell was sweet and alluring. It brought a number of good memories back to his mind. He hadn't even noticed that his eyes had closed as he breathed the aroma.

"Thank you." Puma said as he nodded his appreciation before he began to leave.

"No worries. The Buffalo Soldiers are always welcome among us. We will aid and assist however we can." The chief replied with a grin. He told one of the younger Indians with him to give Rude Boy two of the squirrels they had caught during the hunt. The young man had about a dozen of them over his shoulder so it wasn't an issue to give away two. Once the squirrels were safely secured onto Rude Boy's horse the Indian Chief lifted his head in acknowledgement of Rude Boy. The gesture was a clear sign of respect that was followed up by him taking his closed fist and using it to beat his chest. All of the other Indians copied his gesture then they bid them a farewell and wished them safe travels. The ride back to camp was a quiet one. Rude Boy was mentally still trying to make sense of the two meetings. The fact that he was still trying to grasp the reality of the fact that he was free didnt make it any easier.

CHAPTER 4

    Back at their camp Blue already had a fire going. He was adding firewood from time to time from a pile of it he kept next to him. Although Texas was hot during the day it became very cold at night. When Rude Boy sat down between Blue and Slim, Blue handed him a stick to add to the fire. His strong face smiled briefly. Rude Boy threw the stick into the fire and he watched as it slowly was consumed by the flames.
    Over the fire was a pot. Slim had caught a few snakes and a rabbit so it was looking like snake and rabbit stew was for dinner. Slim noticed the squirrels and he told them that they would come in handy. He immediately started adding them to the meal. Puma was busying himself by rolling the ganja in a piece of tobacco leaf as he prepared to smoke. He licked the blunt he had created to seal its contents. Rude Boy looked at Blue again who was now staring up into the night sky with a blank look on his face. Rude Boy couldn't help wondering what he was thinking and what he was looking at so he looked up too. In the night sky there was a full moon. Its glow seemed almost magical.
    "It's beautiful." Rude Boy commented.
    Blue glanced in his direction and nodded before turning his attention back to the light in the sky.
    "How did you come to become an outlaw?" Rude Boy asked him. Blue looked at him again but this time he frowned. His entire visage was covered in sadness. He wondered what memory he just reawakened in his mind with that question because it was obvious that it caused him some sort of pain to think about it. He waited for a reply that didnt come and he was about to ask him again but Slim intervened.
    "Blue doesn't talk." Slim told him.

"Doesn't talk?" Rude Boy was confused.

"Ever."

Rude Boy looked at Blue who had once again returned his gaze to the night sky. The look on his face was almost absent as if he was there with them only in flesh and blood. His mind was elsewhere.

"How does that work?" Rude Boy asked.

"Sometimes you don't need words to communicate." Puma said suddenly. "Blue is family and that's all that matters. Him knows this like we know this. What's understood doesn't have to be explained. Kind of like how you knew you would be better off with us versus staying with the pale skins."

Rude Boy nodded. He watched as Puma carefully lit the hand rolled joint from the fire. Then he hit it a few times inhaling it deeply in through his mouth before releasing it through his nose. Rude Boy couldn't help mentally likening the sight to that of an angry bull. He inwardly smiled at the thought. The smoke from the joint was very different. He had never smelled anything like it. He had smelled tobacco burning on multiple occasions. The white man smoked tobacco regularly but this was something of its own. He disliked the smell of burning tobacco but he couldn't say the same for whatever substance he was burning in the joint he had hand rolled. He was so caught up in his own thoughts that he hadn't even realized that he had been staring at him the entire time. Puma smiled at him as he held the joint out for him to take.

"You want to smoke?" He asked him.

"No, no,no." He replied quickly. The thought had never crossed his mind although he did notice that it smelled good. "I was just wondering how you got your name but it does smell good." He admitted.

"You want to know how I got my name?"

"Yes sir."

"Then hit the blunt and don't call me sir again. That comes from that slave business. None of that here. We are all family now. You call us by name and by name only. The only exception to that is family or brethren. Ya hear?" He forced the blunt into Rude Boys hands. He held it awkwardly. He looked from the blunt back to him again.

"Ok but how did it happen?" Rude Boy asked.

"Hit the blunt!." Puma yelled at him suddenly. The sudden and sharp command caught him by surprise. Rude Boy immediately did as he was told. It wasn't as if he was acting out of fear. It was more out of respect than anything. He raised the blunt to his lips and pulled on it bringing the sweet smoke into his lungs. He immediately blew it out again before repeating the action once more.

"What are you doing mon!"Slim cried suddenly.

Rude Boy looked confused. He glanced at everyones face before looking back at Slim. "What?" He asked him. He didn't know what was going on. "I'm smoking."

"The horse's ass. That's not smoking. What you're doing is called wasting good ganja."Slim told him. He looked toward Puma to see if what he was saying was the truth or if he was just pulling his leg.

"He doesnt lie to you."Puma told him.

"What do you mean? I'm smoking, see." Rude Boy told them as he repeated the process again by inhaling the smoke again before letting out a steady stream of smoke from his lips.

"No you're not. You aren't even inhaling the smoke. You are literally wasting it. You need to inhale the smoke. You just keep blowing it out." Puma told him, causing Slim to laugh heartily. He laughed so hard he had to fight for breaths just to speak.

"Him a rookie. I can tell that this is the mon first time smoking." Slim added. He shook his head knowingly.

"Hit the blunt and then I want you to open your mouth while the smoke is still in there. That's when you inhale deeply. Once you do that I want you to just hold the smoke there for as long as you can. Ya hear?"Puma directed him.

Rude Boy did as he was told and then Slim took it from him and started smoking too. When Rude Boy finally exhaled the smoke, he was coughing up a storm that made all three of them laugh. He continued to cough as the blunt went in rotation and Slim patted him on the back roughly.

"Keep smoking like that and you might make me think you have Indian chief blood running through your veins."Slim joked." Now all you need to do is learn to breathe again."

"Yes, you will learn to chief yet." Puma told him as the blunt was returning to him after making it through their small rotation. He hit the blunt. He started to let the smoke out of his mouth but he pulled it back in then released it from his nostrils. A light chuckle escaped Rude Boys lips as he watched the man smoke. The sight reminded him of an angry bull. His laugh caught Pumas attention and he suddenly was holding the blunt out in Rude Boy's direction again but this time he was holding in the smoke from his second hit as he had told Rude Boy to do earlier. Rude Boy had to decline. He shook his head as he continued to cough up flem. Slim laughed as he took the blunt instead.

"Why do they call you Puma?" Rude Boy found himself asking before he even knew what he was doing. It seemed the effects of the ganja were beginning to hit him. He was starting to feel weird but in a good way. It was hard to explain. All he knew was that he felt relaxed. He repositioned himself on his rock so that he was more comfortable.

"I am the fastest gun in the whole wild wild west, ya hear me? Fast like a puma. Mon don't disrespect me or my gang. They fear the Dreads. Mon dread to cross paths with The Dreads. You are a Dread now too. Them shall fear you as well.

"Wunna gonna have to let your hair loc and grow now that you are a Dread. You are never to cut it again. That is a part of our way of life." Puma told him.

Blue offered the blunt to Puma again but this time he denied it. He didn't deny it because he couldn't handle it anymore. He denied it because he was interested in the young man before him.

"Me school this youngblood right here." He told Blue and Slim as he turned his attention back to Rude Boy. "Pale skins make you cut your hair because they know what it symbolizes. They know the importance of it. We weren't meant to cut our hair. Listen to me closely now. Our hair is our strength. You have been cut off from the truth. We are descendants of kings and queens. This is my crown." Puma said as he pointed towards his hair.

"We are Dreads. Our people are the only people that can have dreadlocks. Our hair is the thickest amongst all people. Thick like wool. Thick hair is strong hair. Strong like our wills. The point is for them to take the hair so that it will make wunna forget how strong wunna really is. Cutting your hair also symbolizes disconnection from one's ancestors. Have you ever noticed how weak and stripped you feel when it is taken? It is a different form of nakedness. The worst if you ask me." Puma told him.

"How long have you been growing yours?" Rude Boy asked him in awe of the knowledge that he was learning. It was a lot to take in at one time but he was absorbing it all like a sponge.

"Since birth." He replied proudly.

He couldn't believe it. Hair cuts were mandatory for him and all slaves once a month but he was used to it because it had been that way since he could remember. Only women were allowed to let their hair grow and sometimes it would be cut as a form of punishment. His hair had never been longer than a small afro his entire life. He had to admit that he did hate haircuts but he had never had a choice to let it grow.

The three black men before him were the first he had ever seen with long hair, but then again they were the first black men he had seen do a lot of things. What he was being told was slowly beginning to make sense to him but it was also a lot to take in at once. Especially coming from where he had come from. It was like today was the first day of his life and he had been reborn as a member of the Dreads. Puma noticed the conflict in his eyes because he had seen it before with Slim and Blue as well. It was easy for him to read people plus he had encountered many blacks like him before. They often looked at him as a deity.

"I was born an outlaw." He began to explain. "My father was an outlaw. He taught me everything I know and I've been blessed to be able to share. Without my father The Dreads would not be. I started the gang long ago. Slim was the first addition and then Blue came. Now you have come into our family as well."

"How did you meet Slim?" Rude Boy asked him.

Puma smiled as he glanced in Slims direction who also grinned briefly. He played with the long hairs that made up his beard as he reminisced.

"I was just a teenager like yourself when I met him. I was sixteen years young then but of course I was already a known outlaw by then. The name Puma already struck fear in the heart of the pale skins." He retrieved a piece of a cut out poster from his pocket. Rude Boy saw that it had a picture of him all alone brandishing a revolver. He also had a wanted poster that showed the trio. He noticed that something had been ripped off of the wanted posters in the same spot on the both of them. It looked like it used to say something because he could see what looked like partial letters.

"What did it used to say?" He asked.

"Dead or Alive. That's what it used to say but they can never have me. I would never surrender. It is what we have in common with the Indians. Our spirit. I learned long ago that I would rather die on my two feet like a man before I would live on my knees, but enough with that. I met Slim through a small tribe of indians. He had been living among them since a baby. The Indians respect our people. Especially those of us that aren't in bondage. They call us Buffalo Soldiers as you saw. It is a sign of respect. You know, buffalos are the only creatures known to man that will run head on into a storm. They face their problems and conquer them. That is the spirit we have within. That is the spirit I see within you my youth. No fear. Me don't fret. Jah is good.

"The Indians are our brethren. Never forget that. They are peaceful but they war with the pale skins because they think they run the world. The earth belongs to no man. It is Jahs. I would purchase ganja from them as we did earlier. They've always burned it as incense in their rituals. The smell is what drew me to them. My mother and father always smoked it in my youth. I remember instantly recognizing the scent. I still don't know why they don't smoke it directly. They don't know what they are missing out on. They are wasting it if you ask me."

"What was Slim doing with the Indians?"Rude Boy asked him.

"His parents were apparently runaway slaves. They left him with the Indians and vowed to return for him when it was safe because they were being pursued by bloodhounds and they didn't want to lead them to their child. They preferred that he get away instead of them all getting caught. This is the story the Indians told him because it was the last time either of them were seen again. The Indians raised Slim well though. He has the spirit of a mountain lion." Puma told him.

"I was taught to be a free spirit. They treated me like family." Slim added to what Puma said.

"Why did you leave?"Rude Boy asked him.

"I met a free man that looked like myself. Why would I stay? I still remember the day. He had long dreadlocks. I had never seen them before and I believe it was one of the reasons I was drawn to Puma. I had long hair too of course because I was living amongst the indians. They are very free spirited people. I had long braids like all of the other Indians but I always had a different type of hair. Puma said that he was a Dread and that I was too by blood. He said I was meant to have hair like him and I heard the truth in his words."

"He used to cough like you did when he first stopped wasting the ganja." Puma laughed.

"That was a long time ago." Slim said as he grabbed the blunt from Blue and made a show of taking a big hit.

"So you and Puma were together already when you met Blue?" Rude Boy asked. Slim simply nodded as he inhaled the smoke.

"We had been together almost two years." Puma started. He exhaled a deep breath as if he was preparing to tell a long painful story. "We were on the road when we passed him on the ground. He was literally covered in blood from the crown of his head to the sole of his feet. He was on top of a pale skin. It looked like he had killed the man with his bare hands. The scene was gruesome. The average stomach would have emptied itself at the sight. It was clear to me what had taken place there. Not far away was a wheelbarrow full of onions. A horse whined closely too. I assume the pale skin was his oppressor and some sort of argument took place while he was working. Blue looked like a zombie when we found him. He was staring off into space. I don't know what he was thinking but I knew I couldn't leave brethren like that.

"He was sitting there looking depressed and blue as if he were waiting to die. Thus his name. I think he felt that it would be useless to run or maybe he was in shock. I can't say for sure that I know. I am sure that he was not expecting us to stumble upon him though. I told him to come with us. I remember talking to him but it was like he hadn't heard a word I said. I started to shake him but as soon as I touched him his head snapped in my direction. He had this look in his eyes like that of a wild animal but it visibly eased when he noticed my skin color. I'm sure my entire person was different to him" Puma said as he spoke of his hair and stature.

"I told him he would have a life with us and he has. We have never heard him even speak a word before but it doesn't matter. Actions speak louder than words and he has been loyal from a fault. Family. That is what we are. We dont know what horrors his eyes have seen before us that caused him to become mute. We don't even know if he has always been a mute. We honestly don't care. He loves us and we love him as is. That is what The Dreads are about. Love. One love. One mind. One people. One blood." Puma told him.

Rude Boy was listening closely. He was trying to soak up every word like a sponge. He saw Puma as the most important male figure he had ever met before. He looked up to him as a role model of sorts. He wanted to live free and be like him.

"One love, One mind, One people, One blood." Rude Boy echoed him. He liked and quickly memorized the mantra.

"Yes brethren." Puma smiled.

"The stew is done." Slim announced after peeking into the pot. He pulled the pot from above the fire and poured everyone a bowl. It was only then that Rude Boy realized how hungry he was. He began to wolf down the bowl so fast that he almost forgot his manners. He told Slim he was grateful for the food but when he looked back at his bowl it was more than halfway empty.

"Slow down Rude Boy." Puma laughed as he was finishing the last of it.

"He eats like he thinks somebody might take the bowl from him at any moment or something." Slim stated jokingly. "Nobody messes with The Dreads' food. Not even the pale skins. Know that. There is plenty. Get more. Get as much as you want."

He didn't have to tell Rude Boy twice. He took Slim's words as an invitation to start serving himself. He ate two more bowls before passing out with his head propped up against the rock he had been sitting on. He had slept in the worst conditions before so sleeping on the rock wasn't uncomfortable to him.

"The ganja put him out like a light." Slim observed.

"That and those bowls of stew will do it." Puma laughed before saying "Rude Boy" under his breath to himself.

That night Rude Boy slept like a baby. He slept so good that he dreamed that Slim was playing a tune with his harmonica. The tune was so melodic that even Blue was lightly whistling along and tapping his foot to it. Then Puma began to sing. 'Say what you wan say, Do what you wan do, Vanity, Its all vanities, Hard work and no play, The fool of all fools, Vanity, Its all vanities.'

CHAPTER 5

Rude Boy woke up that morning to see the sun shining brightly in his eyes. He immediately tried to shield his eyes from the strong rays of light. Then he was nudged. He originally thought the sun had awoken him because the heat had him drenched in sweat. He quickly learned he had been awakened by the source of the nudging when he turned over and tried to return to his slumber. He saw Puma leaning over him with a very serious look upon his face. Rube Boy sat up instantly.

"You smell that?" Puma asked him as he wrinkled his nose. Rude Boy was lost though. He didn't smell anything. He looked around noticing Slim and Blue were also already awake. He didn't see a look of alarm on any of their faces although he seriously didn't think there was anything that would cause The Dreads discomfort. He looked back at Puma with confusion written all over his face.

"Breathe the air Rude Boy and you will see. Inhale, exhale." Puma told him as he took a deep breath himself. Rude Boy followed suit. He thought he was going to smell smoke in the distance or a rancid smell but he couldn't smell anything but the fresh air around him.

"That is freedom that you are smelling right there. You like it?" Puma asked him.

Rude Boy nodded quickly as he caught on. He had just spent his first night as a free man.

"You want to keep your freedom?" Puma asked him. Rude Boy nodded again.

"You have to be willing to fight for it every second of every day for the rest of your life. There are those that would wish to take our freedom away from us. Those are enemies of The Dreads. You will fight with me against them?"

"Yes. I will." Rude Boy said verbalizing his agreement this time.

"Good, very good." Puma smiled. "Let me tell you a story. You see this handkerchief around my neck? Do you know what it symbolizes?" He pointed to the dark blue handkerchief that he was wearing. Rude Boy shook his head no after examining it from a distance.

"What color is the sky?" Puma asked him

"Blue." Rude Boy answered him thinking it was a trick question.

"Correct. The sky has no limits nor any boundaries. It is free to be what it has always been. This handkerchief was my fathers. He was a free man. He told me that the color blue is a symbol of freedom. The birds fly free in the blue sky. It is true." Puma passed a torn piece of paper to Rude Boy he had pulled from his pocket. He unfolded it and realized that the worn piece of paper was an old wanted poster. The poster depicted the picture of a black man with dreads that were just past his shoulders. The man closely resembled Puma but he could tell it wasn't him. This man was larger than Puma and his facial hair grew differently than his as well. Plus the wanted poster read 'Jamaican Jack' 'wanted dead or alive'.

"My father wasn't born an outlaw like I was. He was born a slave until he ran away. He escaped not long after the slave ship he was on arrived here from an island in the Caribbean known as Jamaica. He became an outlaw, murdering to keep his freedom and robbing to survive. It is nothing that the pale skins don't do as well. Once he even said that we have more in common with the pale skins than many wish to admit. I asked him what he meant by that and he told me that all life comes from one source. The spirit is a mysterious thing he said.

"My father used to say that the only way to have true peace was to be war ready. Anyways, this is an old picture compared to the last time I saw him. His dreads had grown to the middle of his back. He stopped robbing and living the life of an outlaw when he met my mother. My mother was a free woman. She worked hard to buy her freedom. They fell in love as soon as they laid eyes upon one another. I've told no one this story before. Not even Blue or Slim." Puma told him as Slim visibly shifted so that he could hear the story better.

Even Blue had stopped stargazing and seemed to be listening closely. "He stopped robbing and living the life of an outlaw when he met my mother. One could say he had become soft but that isn't how I saw things. I can agree that he let his guard down but that's about it. You see, my mother began to enlighten him on our true history as a people. She wanted to return to Africa where we all come from. She came from Jamaica as a free woman so she and my father had a lot in common considering he had been born on the island too, although he had been born into slavery.

"They spoke highly of the island and its beauty but her agenda was based on eventually returning to our true homeland. She was big on culture. My father said she was the one who told him the truth about our hair. They had their own cabin and everything. I was born of their union right in it. My mother didn't eat meat either. She said it was not a part of our true way of life. Man was meant to live in harmony with all life but I haven't kept true with that since her passing. Neither did my father."

Suddenly Puma's whole mood shifted and he seemed somber as he continued on with his story. "My mother changed my father. She helped pay for his free papers and everything. He had begun to earn an honest living too. He worked as a cow hand until they came for him. Meat wasn't the only thing he gave up. He thought he had buried Jamaican Jack but one day a group of pale skins came for him with this very wanted poster. They burned down our cabin and killed my mother.

"They killed my mother that day and would have killed my father and me as well if they could have. My father had brought me out to work that day and was showing me the trade when he spotted the smoke. He knew instantly where it was coming from so we rushed home but it was too late. She was already dead and they had burned the house down too with her in it. That day Jamaican Jack was reborn. I was only three years young.

"He became a real militant after that and he taught me to be that way too. He taught me that one must always fight for their freedom and that you can never get comfortable. We are at war for peace of mind. Never forget that my youth. The day you forget to fight is the day that someone will be right there waiting to take it all away. The enemy comes to steal, kill and destroy." Puma wiped a lone tear away.

"My father was killed in a shootout when I was six. I saw him drop dead right before my eyes. I had seen death before on many occasions by then but it hits different when it's one of yours doing the dying. His death made me the last of kin in my family. He was my protector but he was gone. I remember how his killer looked at me after shooting my father in the throat. I ran in fear. It was only by the grace of Jah that i wasn't captured and sold into slavery. I Had my fathers handkerchief and one of his guns but I still ran. He taught me how to shoot and everything but when it came time to use it, I didn't even have the heart to attempt to avenge my father.

"I lived on my knees for almost an entire year after that. Maybe that is why I felt sympathy when I saw you. Maybe it is why I brought Blue along. I know what it feels like to live below the standard of life.

I felt all alone like Slim did amongst the Indians as I went from town to town begging and stealing to survive. When i look back at it i can't say it was even living. Now that I know what life means I stand firm on my belief and I felt it was my duty to share it in some way.

"I remember the first day I made it up in my mind that I couldn't live like that anymore. I remember it like it was yesterday and I always will. I remember I used to have nightmares about my fathers death. I watched him die because he was a little slower on the draw than the next man. He died because he was too slow. I remember making a vow to him to become the fastest gun slinger in the wild west. He named me Puma, a creature known for its speed. I vowed to my father that I would bring honor to the name he had bestowed upon me.

"Not even an hour after making that vow I was tested. I was passing through a town when a pale skin pushed me out of his way. I gunned him down on the spot. I have left a trail of blood behind me ever since. You understand?"

Rude Boy nodded.

"So what are you willing to do to keep your freedom?" Puma asked him as he stood up straight and examined Rude Boy.

Rude Boy stood to his feet and wiped as much dust off of him as he could in one swipe. "Fight." He said as he positioned his feet as if he was willing to throw down right there. "I'm going to fight till my last breath."

Puma smiled at him. He was clearly impressed by Rude Boys' energy. "I know you will Rude Boy. I know you will fight to the best of your natural ability but will it be enough? You are very small. I highly doubt you could kill a man with your bare hands like Blue did. I honestly don't think it would be much of a task for an adult pale skin to overpower you. You are still young and you may just grow to be very strong one day but right now strength isn't your key."

Rude Boy looked over himself. He hadn't thought about that. He just knew he didn't want to return to how he had been living before meeting The Dreads. He agreed with Puma on the point that it wasn't living at all in his opinion. Puma suddenly pulled a pistol from his waist. It was the same one he had taken from the guard at the bank. Rude Boy recognized it because it was newer than the other pistols he had. He handed it to him. Rude Boy twirled the pistol in his hands as he examined it. It was the first one he had ever held before.

"I was seven when I killed a man for the first time. I was even smaller than you are now. It made the others think twice about messing with me. They don't want to die either. All creatures cling to life. It is a part of our natural instincts. Being so small I constantly had to kill but eventually word of who I was quickly spread and people began to dread the name and sight of me. They began to think twice about taking my freedom. The cost for attempting to do so was too dire. Like I said, you are bigger than I was back then but they will still test you. You must be ready to defend your freedom with deadly force." Puma told him.

Puma showed him how to hold the gun properly and how to pull the trigger. It all seemed simple enough. Point and pull. Puma then pointed to a cactus a few yards away and told him to shoot it. Rude Boy did as he was told. He put the cactus in his sights and squeezed the trigger. The gun jerked ever so lightly in his hands but he still noticed the force of the shot. The sound of the gun going off surprised him too. It was very loud. He looked in Pumas' direction.

"Don't look at me. You need to be looking at that cactus. That's why you didn't hit the damn thing."Puma scolded him.

Rude Boy aimed at the cactus again and pulled the trigger again and again. He missed shot after shot, becoming frustrated. He shot until Puma told him to stop after almost emptying the pistol.

"You still missed. How old are you right now?"Puma asked him.

"Thirteen."Rude Boy replied.

"I had better aim than you at the age of three years young." He laughed heartily before suddenly becoming serious again. "Your aim is vital in your survival. You now only have one more bullet in that pistol. That cactus doesn't even move and you can't hit it. How do you expect to be able to hit a moving target? You need to concentrate. I know you can do better than you've been doing. Don't think too much. Let your instincts lead you. You won't always have me around."

Rude Boy aimed at the cactus again concentrating before he pulled the trigger. He breathed in deeply and exhaled his breath as he relaxed himself just before the shot. He put a clean hole just in the top of the cactus. It was smoking briefly. Puma nodded subtly. Then he showed him how to empty the pistol and how to reload it as well. He told him that the process of loading and unloading other pistols would be similar to what he had just done if not the same. He said he would teach him to operate a rifle later but for now knowing how to use a pistol was important. It would be his primary weapon.

He had six shots in his pistol. He told him it was important to always keep count. A fatal mistake would be to think you had another shot when you really didn't. Once the pistol was loaded again Rude Boy pointed it at the cactus ready to shoot again but Puma stopped him.

"What are you doing? You've learned enough. Load, shoot, unload then reload." Puma told him as he saddled his horse. Slim and Blue followed suit as well. "Do you think bullets grow on trees or something?

"Another thing. Do you know why we call ourselves outlaws? It isn't just something that we are called. It actually is our way of life. The term comes from the fact that we do not consider ourselves under the laws that man has established. Contrary to what many may believe, we do not consider ourselves to be above the laws of man either. We live our lives outside of the laws that man has established. That is why we have been coined outlaws. We are governed by Jahs law and no other, ya hear?

"The pale skins believe that I am the leader of The Dreads but that is not true. I just let them believe as they will. I am shown respect by my brethren for having lived our way of life for the longest amount of time among us. I am respected for sharing my knowledge. The truth is that we are led by the spirit and the spirit only."

CHAPTER 6

"We are going to have to get you your own horse. You are a man now. Every man should have his own horse." Puma told Rude Boy who held onto him as they were riding into town. They were just behind Slim and Blue. They met Blue and Slim at the edge of town. They all dismounted their horses as they entered the town. The town was mostly quiet considering it was just past noon. Rude Boy kicked a tumbleweed as it was rolling past him along the ground.

In front of a baby blue two story Victorian home a white man sat on his porch steps smoking a tobacco pipe. He looked to be about in his late thirties early forties. On the side of the steps was a wheelbarrow full of pears. Next to the wheel barrow were two barrels. One of the barrels contained onions and the other one contained potatoes.

"We got what you needing. Onions, potatoes,and fresh pears. The pears are just in from California. They are my juiciest batch yet." He boasted as he saw them walking up his street.

Puma handed Rude Boy a potato sack and told him to fill it with pears. Rude Boy happily obliged. He had never had pears before and he wondered how they would taste. He imagined how juicy they would be as he placed the pears into his sack one after the other.

"That's a lot of pears, little feller. Looks like you're about to buy me out. How are you going to pay for all of that?" The man asked him as he sat up straight on the porch.

The man's words shocked Rude Boy as they registered in his mind. He had not even thought about that. He had no money and Puma hadn't given him any either. He noticed that Puma,Slim and Blue hadn't even missed a step. Puma had told him to get the pears and that was that. Now he began to wonder if he was expected to steal the pears. He quickly reasoned against the last thought because stealing them would have been virtually impossible with the man sitting just before the pears. He assumed he was supposed to take the pears. Considering the fact that he was an outlaw now, it all made sense. That's what the outlaws did. They were free to do as they wished. May the Lord be with those who stood in the outlaws' way. He turned his back to the man and ignored him as he continued to fill his sack.

"I said how are you going to pay for all that?" The white man demanded as he quickly came to Rude Boys side. He grabbed a hold of his wrist as he was grabbing another pear. The man had a vice grip on him. He couldn't go anywhere. He squeezed so hard on his wrist that he was forced to drop the pear he was holding. It hurt as he tried to pull away. Rude Boy glanced in the direction of The Dreads but they didn't seem to even notice what was taking place. It looked like they were busy discussing the first place they wanted to visit in the town.

"Let go of me!" Rude Boy cried as he futilely struggled to free himself. The man had a good grip on his only free hand while the other one still held the sack he had filled with pears. Rude Boy watched the man's face as it began to transform into a wicked smile.

"It's a crime to steal, you know. Now what should I do with a thief like you? That's not really my department honestly. I'll just have to let the sheriff decide." The man told him as he began to squeeze even harder on his wrist.

Slim was pointing to a bar near the center of town. "They will probably have a decent meal and a strong drink inside."

"We can check it out for sure." Puma agreed. The sound of a gunshot surprised them. They glanced in the direction they heard it ring out from. When Puma turned around Rude Boy was standing right next to him. He had the potato sack in one hand and his pistol in the other. He held the bag out to him and Puma saw that the sack was full of potatoes like he had thought it would be. Puma looked down the street behind Rude Boy and he saw the man who had been selling the pears was holding his bleeding arm where he had been shot.

"He shot me! The nigger shot me! He is a filthy thief! Someone please help me! Call the Sheriff and arrest him!" He cried drawing the town's attention. People began to come to their doors and some looked from their windows. It was clear the town wasn't used to this type of excitement.

"He was trying to take my freedom." Rude Boy explained to Puma with apparent fear in his eyes. He didn't want to be arrested. He wanted to stay free. Puma told him not to fret and that he ought to stay cool, calm and collected. He crouched down so that he was eye to eye with him before speaking again.

"That was a test of heart, family. You have the spirit of a lion, you hear? Dont let no one steal your glow. You did good protecting yourself but now you need to pay attention." Puma told him before standing back up. He used his hand to indicate the people that had been drawn to the commotion the man was making. Lastly he pointed out the man that Rude Boy had shot in the arm. The man was still complaining about being robbed and shot.

"You hurt him good but maybe some of these other pale skins don't mind getting hurt to take away your freedom. At the end of the day all you did was hurt him and he will heal in time and be good as new. You dead him and they will think twice. No one wants to die before their time, you hear?" Puma told him.

"What?" The white man who was shot said as he overheard what Puma was saying. It sounded to him that the older man had just told the younger to kill him in so many words. Rude Boy immediately heard the same thing as well. He didn't want the other bystanding pale skins to try to arrest him. They greatly outnumbered him so there was only one logical decision to be made. What would happen if they caught him? He imagined unthinkable tortures just before his death. The chills ran through his body first followed by anger. He became angry at the thought of what they would do to him and instinctively his gun came up in the direction of the man he had already shot once. The man ran and scrambled to get back inside his home. Puma put his hand on Rude Boy's hand with a smile as he stopped him from shooting him.

"Keep the pears!" The man yelled back to them as he locked his door.

"You did good. Next time just make sure you shoot to kill. Don't waste a bullet." Puma told him. Rude Boy nodded. Puma reached into the bag and retrieved a pear that he handed to him.

"Thank you." Rude Boy said as he took a bite.

"You deserve it." Puma told him.

"What is all this commotion in my town about?"

The loud commanding voice had everyone's attention. It came from a sheriff who was approaching them on horseback. The sheriff dismounted his horse towards the front of their group where Slim stood defensively. He was closely followed by a younger deputy of his. The sheriff let his hand rest on the pistol in its holster at his hip. Slim instinctively began to reach for his pistol but Puma told him to chill and that he wanted to hear what the sheriff had to say.

"Dammit." Slim complained as he obeyed Puma. "It seems like I will never get to have any fun anymore."

A RUDE STORY

The sheriff surveyed the situation with his eyes before he spoke. "I am sheriff T. Swain and as the Sheriff of this town I am charged with keeping the peace. Me and my deputy here want no trouble but I am going to have to ask you gentlemen to leave."

Slim's hand now firmly rested on his pistol again and he was looking to Puma for the signal.

"I got this." Puma told Slim before throwing him a pear. Slim made a show of taking a bite of the pear as he watched the sheriff before making way for Puma. Puma walked slowly and methodically towards the sheriff. He tossed the sack of pears to Blue and told him to get one. He was cool,calm and collected as he continued to approach the sheriff. He didn't even pay the young deputy any mind. The deputy was young and afraid. Puma could tell because everytime he glanced in his direction he would avoid eye contact. He also kept his hand far away from the pistol at his hip.

Pumas' confidence made the sheriff nervous. He began to sweat and it was only in part because of the Texas heat and the fact that he was slightly overweight. He had a big beer belly that hung out in front of him over his belt. He could blame the town's bar for his beer belly. They took care of him because of the security he provided. Puma stopped just in front of the sheriff.

"What did you say to me and my brethren? I couldnt hear you clearly from afar." Puma spoke slowly to make sure the sheriff understood him. He took a bite from the pear he had in his hand.

"I am Sheriff T. Swain and I am going to have to ask you boys to leave." The sheriff repeated himself just above a whisper that was almost inaudible. None could hear what he had said except for Puma. The sheriff's eyes were somewhere on the floor as he spoke.

"Look at me, ya hear?" Puma told him. He waited for him to look him back in the eyes before he spoke again. "The only reason why you are still breathing is because you asked me."

The sheriff's eyes dropped to the ground again after seeing murder in the black outlaws eyes. He felt like he was being scolded like a child. His eyes eventually returned to Puma.

"I am Puma. Remember that name. No one tells me what I can or can not do and that goes for me and my posse. I am a sovereign. Do you have any idea what sovereignty is?"

He paused briefly, not giving the sheriff a chance to answer the question. "I am free to do as I wish. We will leave this town when we are ready and that is settled. If you ask me to leave again it will be done with your last breath." Puma started to turn around and leave but he quickly spined back to the sheriff. "When I think about it, don't say a thing to me again! I don't want to hear your voice! I've already killed four sheriffs. Please be number five." Pumas' voice carried throughout the streets as his voice raised. It was Rude Boys first time seeing him angry but the funny thing about it was he didnt actually seem angry. He spoke louder but it seemed that he was actually only telling the sheriff the truth. He seemed like the quiet before the storm.

"I don't like your face fella." Puma told him as his voice again mellowed out. His eyes showed his murderous intent if he were to be challenged. Rude Boy thought he looked like a lion. When his voice was raised it reminded him of a roaring lion. The sheriff slowly turned away and mounted his horse without a word. His deputy was frozen still from the shock until Puma looked in his direction. He practically ran to remount his horse and get out of there. Puma stood there and watched as they left. Neither of them looked back even once.

"You good brethren?" Slim asked him as he came to his side.

"Everything criss." Puma smiled as he returned to his normally charismatic self again. Rude Boy started to ask who Chris was but he quickly decided against that as he realized what he had meant. He was learning to understand them despite their heavy accents and frequent use of slang.

"What's the plan?" Slim asked him.

"We still have to see the bar." Puma replied as he led the way to the bar.

CHAPTER 7

    Puma led the gang into the bar after tying their horses up outside. They went straight to the counter. They all followed Pumas lead by taking seats on stools at the counter. Rude Boy noticed the bar was primarily empty save for the squirrely looking young white man at a table in a corner.
    "I need shots for all of my brethren. We are celebrating a new edition to the family." Puma said. The bartender grabbed three shot glasses and filled them up. He passed them to Puma, Slim and Blue. He observed Rude Boy thinking he was too young to drink but he decided against saying something because everyone in the group was armed and he could tell this wasn't a nice gang of people. He heard the commotion earlier and he already knew they were outlaws of some sort.He had seen his fair share of outlaws but these were the first black ones he had ever seen and they had strange hair.
    "Who's paying for all of this?"The bartender asked Puma against his better judgment. Slim laughed suddenly as if he had told a joke.
    "Why didn't you make a shot for Rude Boy? He is my brother too." Puma nodded in Rude Boy's direction so he knew who he was talking about. The bartender glanced at their guns again and he raised his hands in surrender. The squirrely young man noticed the interaction between the bartender and The Dreads and he took it as his sign to get out of there.
    "I don't want any trouble." Is all the bartender said before moving to fix another shot. He placed the shot glass in front of Puma who he took to be the leader. Puma pushed the shot glass in Rude Boy's direction and he insisted that he drink because they were celebrating. He did so and the liquid burned his throat as he chugged it all down in one gulp like he saw the others doing. It tasted like liquid fire.

"It will put hair on your chest." Puma told him and Slim chuckled.

"Think it will take a few more of those to put a hair on that chest." Slim laughed. "Or maybe more than a few."

"We have the whole place surrounded! Come out with your hands up and we won't shoot!" The yell came from the street just outside of the bar. The voice sounded familiar. "This is sheriff T. Swain!" The man yelled to make sure his presence was known. Rude Boy knew he had recognized the voice as soon as he heard it. It was the same sheriff from earlier. He had a feeling that the man would return and he was sure he brought reinforcements this time.

"Surrender and your life will be spared! I count twenty armed men on my side and there are only three of you and a little boy. Be smart about what you do from here!" He yelled. Outside sheriff T. Swain was smiling as he straightened his shirt. He just knew that the small group of outlaws were about to surrender. There was no way they could win a gunfight. They were heavily out gunned and they wouldn't be able to escape on their horses either because of the fact that their horses were in the front of the bar by its only exit and they had that completely covered.

"Seems the sheriff has found his voice." Slim chuckled. "What do you do?" He asked Puma.

"Another round." Puma told the bartender who obliged silently. He calmly knocked back a shot then stood as he headed to the bar's exit. Without saying a word to the gang he walked straight outside without an ounce of fear in him. Slim and Blue followed closely with Rude Boy picking up the rear. His little heart was thumping like a marathon runner's feet against the ground. White men were on both sides of the bar when they exited. There were even a few women in the ranks as well. They had pistols and rifles leveled in their direction.

"You know who I am!" Puma yelled into the man's face. The sheriff's hand rested on his pistol but he didn't dare to draw it. " I am the fastest gun slinger in the wild wild west. Fast like a puma. This is my name by birth." Puma left from in front of the sheriff and began pacing back and forth in front of him and his deputy. He was livid from the presence of the men that had come to oppose him. He was so angry that his eyes turned red. He glanced into the eyes of the deputy standing just behind the sheriff. He seemed to have worked up the courage to let his gun hand rest on his pistol but as soon as Puma and his eyes connected, he moved his hand as if the pistol were a hot stove. Puma looked over all the people that were surrounding them with a menacing stare. Still yet to even reach for his pistol.

"You don't want to rump with Puma! You don't want to rump with The Dreads at all! Wunna make me raise Cain, ya hear? You blood clot pussy wat batty boys know better than to test me! You went and got a mob like I fret them. Me don't care about nothin. I was born for dead. I am ready to dead anything standing in my way so I advise wunna to steer clear."

Blue watched on with a mean look on his face as he fingered the pistols at his waist. Slim Smiled devilishly in a show of cockiness. For a moment Rude Boy thought they were going to all get on their horses unchallenged and ride up out of there but that isn't what took place. The sheriff no longer seemed to have a dog in the fight when Puma called his bluff. That's when a young white man ran up to take the sheriff's place at the head of the mob.

Rude Boy recognized the white man as the overseer Timmy from the plantation he was raised on. Then he noticed a few familiar faces from his past. They seemed to have come to join the mob to specifically apprehend him and take down The Dreads. That very realization had him shaking in fear. He had a feeling things weren't about to turn out too good. Timmy stopped only a few yards in front of Puma in a shooting stance. The sheriff took that as his chance to get out of there and withdraw to the mob behind them.

"Aint no nigger hand faster than this here white hand and thats the God honest truth. I guarantee that." Timmy told him as he spit a glob of chewing tobacco onto the ground. "Fastest gun hand in the west my ass." He mocked him.

Puma inhaled and exhaled as he faced him, keeping his composure. "Reach and you are a dead mon." He told him calmly. All around them the white people had lowered their guns to see what would happen. Standoffs and shootouts were iconic moments in the west that none wanted to miss. Many shootouts and standoffs are still talked about to this day. Everyone liked an old fashioned shootout. The tension was there. You could've heard a mouse piss on tumbleweed.

Timmy's hand hovered just above his pistol. His fingers fluttered as he anticipated pulling his gun. It looked as if he was playing an invisible piano with his hands. His fingers wiggled strangely and suddenly his gun was out in his hand and it was pointed in Pumas' direction. Everything happened so fast. The loud boom of a gunshot didn't make it any easier to discern what had taken place. Rude Boy looked at Puma whose gun was now out as well and it was pointed back at Timmy. He saw a thin line of smoke rising from Pumas' gun barrel. When he looked back at Timmy he had dropped his weapon and was clutching the bleeding hole in his throat where he had just been shot. He fell to his knees first before finally dropping dead in the street.

"Fast like a Puma." Puma said as he glanced back in Rude Boys direction. He was actually smiling. With everything going on Rude Boy couldn't believe he was smiling. "Bet he wont talk like that to me again." he joked, making light of the situation.

"Timmy!" Someone yelled from the mob and then an eruption of gunfire followed. The mob clearly wasn't happy about the outcome of the shootout. Needless to say chaos ensued. Puma turned and immediately returned fire. He made every shot he took count. Every time he fired a shot someone either dropped dead or was knocked down. He hit a man holding a rifle and then hit another with a shotgun. He went to shoot a third person but was hit in the shoulder making his shot a miss. He was such a good shooter that he still hit his target but he only hit that person in the arm. Blue and Slim didn't need to be told what to do. They joined in as soon as the mob started shooting too. They were all excellent shooters but they were badly outnumbered from two different sides.

Someone had shot and killed one of The Dreads horses and it had fallen dead in the street. Rude Boy was using its dead body to shield himself from the gunfire all around. Blue had rushed to Pumas' side and was returning fire. They had just transformed the street into a battlefield. Blue stood in front of Puma as he fired round after round and shielded him from the onslaught of gunfire.

Blue took bullet after bullet protecting Puma. His big frame wasn't easy to take down but it was definitely an easy target. It was hard to miss him and as soon as he came into play all eyes were on him. He made sure to shoot a few of the mob members before he finally collapsed to the ground lifeless. His actions enabled Puma to be able to make it to safety. He joined Rude Boy behind the fallen horse. They were primarily safe from gunfire. A few shots hit Pumas' exposed leg. The dead horse's body continuously took bullet after bullet as they sat there on the ground leaned against the carcass.

Seeing Blue's dead body enraged Slim. He had already killed about five of the men but now he wanted them all dead. He didn't think and he didn't blink. He shot the last two rounds out of his two six shooters, killing another man before rushing a man with a rifle in his hands. His sudden rush shocked the man and it was evident by his wide eyes as he fumbled with the rifle to shoot. He chucked his empty pistol at the man and he just barely dodged. He wasn't able to dodge the second pistol that was launched at his head though.

That was all the distraction that Slim needed. He was up on the man before he could react. He used one of his hands to redirect the

A RUDE STORY

rifle away from him as he punched him in the face. The rifle went off but it didn't hit him. Slim followed up by disorienting him with a elbow to the face that made it easy for him to tear the rifle from his hands. He hit him in the face with the butt of the rifle and knocked the man out cold.

He quickly aimed his rifle at one of the many targets around him. He shot and killed one. As he was taking sight of another target he was hit. He rolled on the ground from the force of the bullet. When he came up onto one knee he shot and killed who had just shot him. He was shot two more times in the back. He lay on the ground as Sheriff T. Swain approached him. He had been staying out of the gunfight until he saw his opening and just couldn't resist.

"It's over." Sheriff T. Swain told him as he kicked the rifle away from Slim's bleeding body.

Slim surprised the sheriff by suddenly rolling over and shooting and killing him with a pistol he had snatched from a dead body. "It definitely is." Slim joked just before getting riddled with bullets by what was left of the mob. His lifeless body was still smiling even after the last breath left him. Rude Boy could hear the surviving white men reloading their weapons after unloading them. It was a horrible sound to recognize.

"The last of the niggers ran behind that horse. Bunch of cowards." Rude Boy heard one of the members of the mob say. He already knew they were pointing to where they hid. Their time was limited until they came for them. Puma was hurt badly and he didn't see himself making it out of this one. He had got hit in the back and it was making it harder and harder to breathe each breath. With both Blue and Slim dead,there was no one to come and save them.

"You good?" Rude Boy asked Puma while fighting back tears. He had seen enough people die to know he wasn't going to make it. He knew he was watching him take his last breaths.

"Everything criss." He said as he glanced at himself. Then he coughed up blood onto his shirt. He moved his jacket to the side and he saw a growing stain of blood on his shirt where he had been hit. He didn't know he had been hit as many times as he had. He had only felt the first time he had been hit. It had been like getting touched with hot coals.

"You're dying." Rude Boy said as he verbalized what he had already figured out. As he spoke he lost control of himself and tears began to fall like rain.

"Cut it out!" Puma snapped. He coughed up blood again then he began to speak to him calmly. "Don't ever let them see you cry. No weakness. They think you are a batty boy if they see you crying.

There are no batty boys in my gang." He started violently coughing up blood again. Rude Boy wiped his eyes on his shirt sleeve and straightened up.

"That's the Rude Boy I know. You like the son I never had. Listen here and listen closely." Puma said coughing in between his sentences. He spoke so low that Rude Boy had to get closer to him to be able to hear him clearly. "They can kill my body but they can not kill my spirit. Thus is the spirit of the Buffalo Soldier. Eternal Life." He laughed and then the light of life in his eyes winked out. He was dead. Rude Boy was all alone again in a cold world.

He heard the mob of men calling out for them from the otherside of the horse's carcass. They mocked them as they cautiously came closer. They taunted them with the most disrespectful words they could think of, hoping to get any type of reaction. Rude Boy was enraged. The mob had just killed the only men in the world that were showing him what it meant to be free. Now they were bragging about doing just that. They were bad men and needed to be taught a lesson.

CHAPTER 8

The last five men approached the dead horse cautiously. They knew these black men to be dangerous savages. There originally had been over twenty of them in the mob when they had begun the shootout against The Dreads. All of their pistols were trained on the horse as they came around it. They found Pumas dead corpse leaning against the horse's underbelly. His eyes were still open but he was blankly staring off into space.

"Damn it! I was looking forward to putting another hot one in him." One of the men commented.

"Shoot him to make sure he's dead then. Can't never be too sure with these crafty devils. I know you saw how that other one popped up like a zombie." Another man suggested. The first man who had spoken started to raise his pistol but sudden movement in his peripheral caught his attention although it was too late. Rude Boy suddenly rolled from underneath the horse's thick thigh. He was so small that it was able to conceal him until the right moment.

All of the men were stunned, giving him the element of surprise. Most of the men flinched. Others froze up. One even fired a reflective shot. Rude Boy had a pistol in both of his hands. He fired at them quickly. He shot from where he lay on the ground at anything moving.

His bullets took the last of the mob of men down one by one. One of them even tried to run after being hit the first time but a bullet caught him square in the back. He clearly wasn't able to outrun a bullet. The street was silent again. Rude Boy unloaded the shells and reloaded his pistols with ease. He straightened the handkerchief around his neck. He had taken it from Pumas corpse and he planned to bring honor to it. He knew he would want him to. His spirit would live on through him.

Even though they had not known each other for a long time, Puma had been like a father to him. He did what fathers do. He taught him what it meant to be a man. It made him feel good to hear him tell him that he had felt the same way.. As a slave, families were often

A RUDE STORY

broken up so he never knew who his father actually was. He used to imagine that his father was some sort of superhero-like character who would one day free him from bondage and now he had Puma.

He knew he carried the same spirit as Puma because he felt the same way that he had. He knew he would rather die on his two feet standing than to ever live another second on his knees again. 'Eternal Life' he thought to himself as he passed the bloody massacre in the streets. He made his way over to the only horse that hasn't been hit by any bullets. It seemed like a miracle. It was the same horse that Puma had ridden. It was visibly shaken up from all of the commotion but it didn't have a scratch on it. He wanted to bury The Dreads dead bodies at first but he decided against it. In his last moments, Puma had told him that his body didn't matter because it was his spirit that would continue to live on. He was sure that Puma, Slim and Blue were watching over him at that very moment. He felt the presence of their spirits. He still remembered the song they had sung in his dream.

He made the horse walk alongside him as he started to leave town. A white man suddenly stirred on the ground near him. It was the same man Slim had knocked out earlier. He might have lived to tell the tale but he had regained consciousness only seconds too soon. The man was groaning in pain. When he noticed Rude Boy watching him, he went for the rifle nearest to him. A shot rang out just as his fingertips were brushing against the gun metal. The bullet found a home in the man's heart. He went limp where he was and Rude Boy's gun was swiftly returned to his side. He left the town without further incident. Those who witnessed everything remained hidden. Fear of a similar demise kept them in place.

ONE WEEK LATER

    In a bank somewhere in Texas a young blonde haired woman wearing a pale blue dress was arguing with her husband as he made a withdrawal.
    "I just have to have the carpet that Jane just made. It is a custom make, made from real bear fur. Everyone in town has one of Jane's carpets except for us. This will be her best work yet though. She told me about it first because I make the best pie and I have been hooking her up. My hard work is finally paying off. She's even giving us a great deal. Don't be a crab honey." The woman cried. "If you get it I promise to show you how much I appreciate you." The woman kissed his earlobe to get her point across.
    "Okay okay." Her husband caved. "Not like I have much of a choice. You'll put a lid on the cookie jar if I don't play along." He muttered under his breath. He told the teller what he needed to withdraw. He was literally about to take out all of his savings for a bear pelt. He shook his head. Love is expensive.
    "What was that?" She asked him.
    "Nothing." He responded quickly. His wife's nose suddenly began to wrinkle up at him and he repeated to her that he hadn't said anything because he thought she was frowning her face up at what he had said under his breath. In all actuality her nose was twitching because of a strange smell that was strong. It caught her attention immediately.
    "What is that?" She asked him again.
    "Nothing honey. I told you I didn't say anything." He repeated again.
    "No. What is that horrible smell?" She turned to look in the direction of the smell. At the bank's entrance she was able to see a young black man as he was dismounting his horse. It was a spectacle to all that saw him. He had a navy blue handkerchief around his neck. He had a small afro that had been parted with rubber bands that would help his hair grow into thirteen locs. He had a hand rolled blunt in his hand that he moved to his lips and took a hit from just as he stepped inside the bank. He created a large smoke cloud that engulfed the woman. She swatted the smoke as she coughed.

A RUDE STORY

"Eww. It stinks. What is that? Don't you know it's rude to smoke inside? I don't want to have to smell that." The woman complained.

"You calling me rude?" Rude Boy laughed.

"Mhmmm. Where are your parents?"

"Slight correction little lady. I'm not just rude. The name is Rude Boy. Rude Boy Dread. Make sure they get it right on my poster." He smiled at the woman mischievously. Her husband pulled his wife into a protective embrace.

"You can't smoke in here." The guard told him as he let his hand rest on the pistol on his hip. He began to size Rude Boy up. It wasn't until he had begun inspecting the young man that he realized he was actually a young boy. He couldn't have been a day older than fifteen. He had absolutely no facial hair. His hand slided away from his pistol as he looked at the man's hair. He had never seen the style before.

"Where's your parents, little boy? You lost?" The guard asked him as he landed a hand onto the young boy's shoulder. He saw the pistol too late. The barrel exploded in the guard's face, dropping him dead on the ground. The woman began screaming loudly and hysterically.

"The name is Rude Boy Dread." He said to the dead man. Then he turned his attention to the teller who immediately threw his hands into the air. "Now you're going to hand over all the money or you'll end up like your friend over here."

THE END